The Woodscrit Manuscripts

Published by Publisher's Cataloging-in-Publication Data
Shoaff, Thomas M.

The Woodscrit manuscripts : a story for children from six to ninety-six / Thomas M. Shoaff and Matthew-John Shoaff. – Fort Wayne, IN : Fox Tale Publishing, LLC, 2008.

p. ; cm.
ISBN: 978-0-9802332-0-9

1. Human-animal relationships—Fiction. 2. Nature stories, American. I. Shoaff, Matthew-John. II. Title.

PS3619.H63 W66 2008
813.6-dc22   2007943422
Aerial photographs by Burnham Graphic Arts
1430 NW Windermere Dr.
Tremont, IL 61568
(309)241-8903

Project coordination by Jenkins Group • www.BookPublishing.com
Interior and Cover design by Barbara Hodge
Prints of art work available at *www.foxtalepublishing.com*

Printed in Singapore
12 11 10 09 08 • 5 4 3 2 1

The Woodscrit Manuscripts

A Story for Children from Six to Ninety-Six

Thomas M. Shoaff

Illustrated by

Matthew-John Shoaff

Fox Tale Publishing, LLC
Fort Wayne, IN

Dedicated to the hallowed tree,
without which there would be no story.

ONCE THERE WAS a deep blue lake surrounded by a land of rolling hills, open meadows and great northern forests, and all this was surrounded on three sides by an even larger and deeper blue lake that stretched from the water's edge to the horizons. The land was inhabited by critters of all manner, large, small and medium, and the critters governed the land through a council of venerated elders, made up of one representative from each species selected from the wisest of the wise and the most just of the just. The critters called this land a "peninsula" and for centuries on end enjoyed its unfailing gifts without intrusion of any kind.

Then one day, the humans came to the peninsula and, try as they might, the critters could not decide what to make of them. So the council of elders devised a judicious plan.

$\mathfrak{T}$HEY WOULD HOLD a council meeting each night, and would send out other critters who were the fastest among them to act as runners, and they would span the peninsula and spy on the humans and take down everything they said and did.

They would then report to the council at dawn, and the elders would select from the reports the most salient passages and inscribe them in woodscrit and keep them in giant tomes for future reference. Thus, if there were ever a problem with the humans, the council could resort to this great body of accumulated knowledge to help them decide how to deal with the humans.

However, to make this work, the elders had to have a properly-suited meeting place. So they determined to seek out the assistance of the grandest and eldest of the ancient timbers that had from time immemorial dotted the peninsula and stood like sentries observing all things past, present and future. One of these was prominent above all others, having preceded the memory of all the critters and even their ancestors, and having captured the legends and traditions of the great peninsula in its numberless concentric rings that measured out its majestic age.

The critter council gave this tree the name of "box elder" because it was the most revered of all the wooded elders, and because it had so graciously offered to host the council and to protect in the ancestral boxes long kept in its lofty halls, the woodscrit manuscripts containing the information that was now to be gathered.

$\mathfrak{T}$ODAY, THERE ARE many box elders, but then there was only one, and every night the council met and heard the reports and made the records that would reside so close to the very heart of the box elder.

And what the council of elders found was that the humans did some things well and others not so well. They built the dam that held the dark blue water in the giant lake that ran the length of the peninsula, which all the critters and the humans loved and that was good, and they built the boat ramps that were used by humans with jet skis who suffered from sensory deprivation and possessed (at best) only the most minimalist of brains, and that was very bad.

THEY BUILT THE vineyards and the cherry orchards that bloomed in spring and blanketed the hills with bright bursting berries in the summer and fall and that was good; and they built the concrete riprap on the shores of the great lake and that was bad.

And so it went, year after recorded year, as their repository of knowledge about the humans expanded, and the critters found that a sort of unspoken balance had been struck between themselves and the humans – whom they nevertheless continued to chronicle in exhaustive detail each day.

The box elder was proud of the service it had been asked to provide, and for years this most assiduous deciduous faithfully and diligently protected the tomes stored in its sacred passageways and willingly served its little masters.

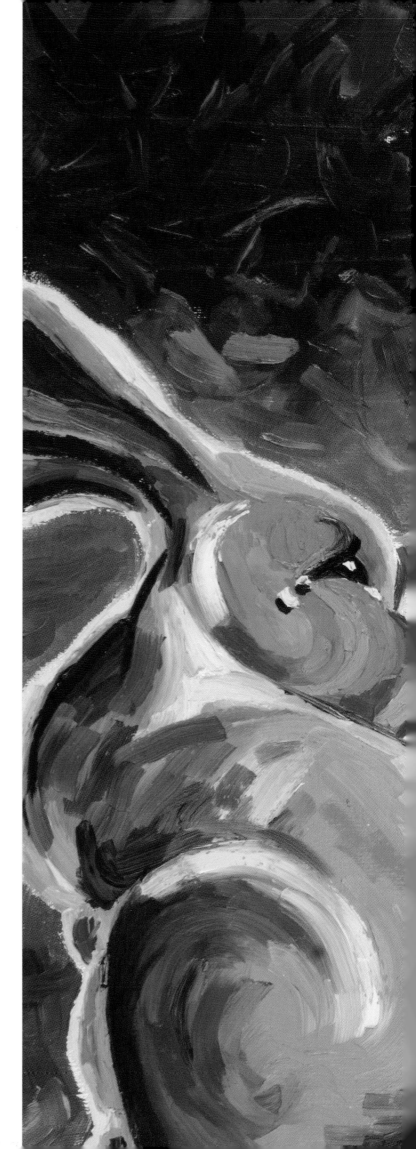

THEN ONE NIGHT, as the box elder was standing up tall and stately against the night wind, the wind whipped into a gale that grew stronger and stronger and fiercer and fiercer until the box elder, which could not bend, was blown over and fell with a great and thunderous crashing sound upon the land. Where this most magnificent of all trees had stood on the horizon was left only a cold grey emptiness in the sky.

6

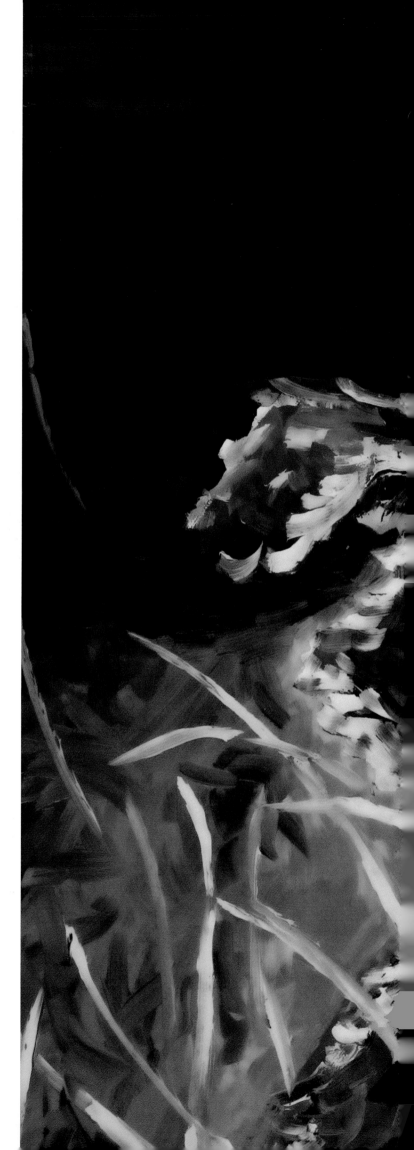

ITH HEAVY HEARTS and more than an occasional tear, which was wiped away quickly so as not to be noticed, the critter council counseled all through the night and into the next afternoon in an attempt to determine what to do about the box elder and its voluminous manuscripts. The little runners, who were less reserved by nature and less able to conceal the great sadness sinking deep within them, huddled together close to the fallen tree throughout the night and the following day and watched in silence, save for the sound of tears steadily falling on the leaves, hoping against hope and praying with all their might that the elders would find some way to fix the mighty box elder.

$\mathfrak{T}$HEN, WITHOUT WARNING, the most unthinkable of all things happened. A man carrying a chainsaw approached the tree and the council of elders knew from now long years of recordkeeping that this could mean no good for their beloved tree.

So the elders summoned up the fastest of all the runners who had served them over the years and one who had observed many humans. This was not only the fastest of the critters, but it was the smallest, and this little critter had an uncommon knowledge about many things and an unerring instinct about some.

This is the one most of all that the elders had listened to intently when the reports were being made, and much of what he reported now fills the tomes. The elders told him he must find the one human on the peninsula who would help save the box elder and there was so little time. The little critter knew that now more than ever, he had to trust his instinct, because only that could direct him to the spot he needed to be in to meet the human he needed to meet to save the box elder.

So he did precisely that and found himself transported swiftly and unfailingly to the appointed place and the person who would understand what he was about to say. The critter said to the human, "You must come with me," and he did.

And when the human saw the man with the chainsaw, he knew why he was there and he said in a level voice, looking straight into the man's eyes, "What are you doing with that chainsaw?" The man replied, "I work for the government and I've come to clean up this messy, disheveled old tree and take its remains to a landfill."

THE CRITTERS' FRIEND then said, "I think not. I'll come back tomorrow and mark this tree with a bright red tape and you can cut everything above the marks I make, but you must leave everything below the marks in tact, and you must not touch the trunk. I will then find a new home for this box elder and you will not have to do a thing."

The man liked his job with the government and thought the only job better than his job was one that involved not working at all, which was a distinction so subtle that few could discern the difference. The government man concluded that this would reduce the work without changing his salary and he readily agreed. It must be said in fairness to the government man, however, that he did not have a bad heart, and may also have thought, with some justification, that to humor the critters' friend while taking credit for removing the tree was a fair bargain for everyone.

THE CRITTERS' FRIEND put a note on the box elder, which he also attached with red tape, and it read, "This tree is being saved for so and so. It will be removed soon." The man later returned to write his name where the words "so and so" had been.

He told the littlest critter to wait patiently for him by the tree and he would set out in great earnest to find a new home for the box elder and would return to tell him what he had found. Within a few days, the man returned and told his little friend that he had found a place across the lake that might be suitable and the council should go there that evening and determine whether they found it agreeable.

THUS, WITH SOME trepidation but stalwart hearts, the elders went to visit this new site and saw that it was at the base of a big hill, and from it, the critters could look out and see the great inland lake that was but a stone's throw away, and this was something they had not been able to do from the old site.

The elders had long known from the ancient lore passed down from council to council, beginning with this, the most important and cherished of all its teachings, that the deepest crevices of the lake reached into the very core of the earth, and that long ago the lake had used these massive and sinewed tentacles to grip the bedrock found there and had anchored the entire peninsula precisely where it was and is, and in that single act had ensured its position as the grandest and most dramatic and, quite simply, most blessed of all the earth's peninsulas.

And, as the elders that preceded them had done, this council of elders held the lake in a special place of reverence for this great and lasting service, and it now seemed to them that the proximity to these inspired waters was an auspicious sign that boded very well for the prospects of the new site.

$\mathcal{A}$ND THE COUNCIL next noticed that on the shore of the lake was a kind of shrine that had two tall pillars at least twice as high as any human they had ever observed and another pillar that went across the top that was as long as the vertical pillars. Below that was another horizontal pillar, and both had curved ends that sloped up to the sky. Inside the shrine hung a perfectly round, massive copper gong that looked out silently over the waters of the great inland lake and the surrounding hills, as though it were the all-seeing eye of the very universe itself. And the critters found that sitting under this lofted and lordly shrine, the world seemed curiously calm, and from it one could watch the sun descend over the horizon and later the northern lights shooting across the sky, and could look straight up and see the big dipper that had intentionally been placed by a provident hand directly over the peninsula to provide a constant evening light for all the critters to see by as they went about their nightly comings and goings.

The council of elders also knew, because other critters had told them, that sometimes the humans rang the big copper gong and it reverberated in waves that reached all up and down the shoreline and even into the deepest recesses of the lake, and the council thought this could come in handy should they ever be required to warn the critters in times of emergency.

This too suggested to the elders that there was something unusually benevolent and critter friendly about this location and they began to feel even more encouraged about the future of these surprising grounds.

And so, when the critters' inspection was finally complete and all these things had been considered, the council concluded that this site had proved to be an unusually hospitable and habitable location and with now ever rising spirits and growing expectations, they told that to the smallest critter who told it to his friend.

The man then went out directly and found some other human friends who had a big flatbed truck and they brought it to where the box elder lay still and ashen as it had fallen.

THEY PUT WIDE straps around the aged tree and gently lifted the tree onto the flatbed truck, and they took it to its new home. There it was lifted by an even larger human contraption by attaching the straps to the mechanism's limbs and then wrapping them around the limbs of the ancient tree, and very carefully placing the tree in a hole big enough to stand the tree straight up and hold it firmly and imperviously against the night wind and all the elements of nature.

𝕴T WASN'T LONG after that that the council of elders was meeting regularly once again in the box elder and recording all that they observed. But the elders found that there was an unexpected bonus that came with this new ground.

As it happened, this land came with a band of boys who returned to the land every summer for a short but glorious time, and these were among the most interesting humans the elders had ever studied. First, they had lots of energy, accompanied by just a touch of whimsy and smattering of foolery, and these things seemed to sustain the boys through most of the night and begin again with each new day. Thus, it was never boring or dull spying on these boys, nor was there ever any shortage of ready volunteers for spying.

During the day, they did all sorts of odd things that all involved a lot of noise and laughter and hooting. One such activity involved a net, and the boys stood on opposite sides and passed things back and forth over the net.

Some were big balls and some were smaller balls with feathers, and the boys took turns jumping up and down wildly, first on one side and then the other, clapping each other on the back and letting out whoops of joy and congratulating themselves on whatever it was that had just happened — but, as the critters keenly noted, no two sides ever seemed to celebrate at the same time.

It was not, at first, clear to the critters how the chatter and whoops and verbal exchanges, which seemed to them quite prolix, related to the purpose of the games or, for that matter, even if the games had a purpose, since whatever objects they were playing with never left the field and therefore never seemed to accomplish much of anything in the end. What was very clear, however, was that no activity could be performed unless all the boys could be heard (almost everywhere) telling all the other boys what they were doing right and wrong and exhorting them to higher and higher levels of rousing effort in what was obviously an Olympic struggle.

24

ONE THAT MUST have had momentous implications for the humans, as all the boys followed their own instructions (and everyone else's) and utterly exhausted themselves before the activity ceased—which it seldom did or, at least, seldom did for long.

Likewise, the critters followed their instructions and wrote it all down as fast as their little paws would allow. It was especially challenging to try to capture the whole of a three thousand or so odd word dialogue offered fervidly, albeit without much organization, by nine or ten urgent contributors in a thirteen minute game, but the critters were pretty sure they got the gist of it—since so much of it was repetitive.

A T NIGHT, THE boys ate and drank enormous amounts of food and beverage (compared to other humans) sitting around a big table under a glass light made to look like brightly colored fruit complete with luscious golden pears, yellow bananas, orange mangos and one outrageous, ruby red pomegranate.

There they took turns (loosely speaking) speaking, after which everybody would laugh and whoop it up some more and add their highly instructive commentaries; and then another boy would say something and the whole place would roar with approval or, occasionally, even deride the luckless speaker mercilessly—which seemed to delight all the other boys even more, and this would continue until much, much later in the evening when finally they concluded it was time to formalize their endlessly spirited goings on.

On some mysterious cue, the boys would then get up and remove themselves to the now long-abandoned boathouse and close its massive accordion doors and overhead windows (as they had been sternly and repeatedly instructed to do), and invited other boys and girls to come too, and they stayed up very late and acted as though they never intended to go to work again. They played music at decibels that ensured that at least the deepest chords of the bass would escape directly through the boathouse walls into the surrounding woods where it could be appreciated as well by the musically inclined critters who might wish to enjoy it—along with those who didn't!

OTHER CRITTERS, TOO numerous to mention by name, positioned themselves around the circular portals of the boathouse where the spying was best and peered down into the din of highly animated and wholly fascinating human activities in full swing below. And, while the critters could not exactly make out what the boys and girls were saying or singing or whooping about, it did seem to them that the humans made less and less sense as the night wore on, and none of them appeared to notice or even care.

As the littlest critter later reported to the council, "The shenanigans just kept burbling out of them without any start or finish whatsoever—like some faucet that won't turn off, no matter how many times you turn it!" And so it was, and as this littlest critter already understood and the elders would later come to understand, this made them just perfect for this most magic of peninsulas.

$\mathfrak{T}$HROUGH IT ALL, the council of elders watched from the elevated vantage point of the sagacious and now much-revived box elder, and the runners watched from inside other old trees and logs and under bushes and peeking over the rooftops. When the boys were inside their shingled cottage, the critters peeked through the windows and knocked each other down trying to get the best seats. Sometimes when the fireplace was not in use, they climbed down the chimney and peeked out from under the grate and didn't mind the soot at all, which made even the non-raccoons look like raccoon cousins with little soot masks outlining their wide, unblinking eyes.

THE CRITTERS GOT so wrapped up in these humans that they looked forward to their coming back every year, and waited impatiently for the glorious days when the boys would arrive to brighten the peninsula and revel in the good nature and delectable buoyancy that came from just being there and being in such good company — which, unbeknownst to the boys, now included a throng of captivated critters, carefully and gleefully inscribing it all for posterity.

As the critters were finding out, there is something about a feeling of goodwill as it settles on a place that makes no distinction between critters and humans and it graces all things equally, and no place was this truer than this most extraordinary of all corners of the earth with its blue-green waters and azure skies. Indeed, when the sun shines on this peninsula, it's as though God's own smile chose this place to rest, and it warms the hearts of every living thing — and maybe, just maybe, that's why this was the perfect place for the little critters to form their silent bond with the boys. Or, perhaps, it was that they just had the same spirits in different guises and this place of miracles let them share it. But whatever its reasons, it just was and that's what was important.

$\mathfrak{A}$T THE END of the first season of memories, the council of elders had wisely assigned each boy his own page in the woodscrit manuscripts and every year the pages got longer and longer, as they filled up with reports of high jinks and endlessly competitive games that no one would concede and each boy took to be the measure of his whole life's worth. Net games and lake games and card games and storytelling – each of which followed the hours of the clock around and around in their own seemingly endless concentric circles. And, of course, every boy was required to master and repeat in staccato fashion, on call, the name of every player that had ever played on any sporting team, at any time, in the history of the country.

These important things found their way into the woodscrit manuscripts again, and again, and again. And when the boys left, the elders and the critters were very sad, but they had their tomes and their memories and their plans for next summer.

In the dead of winter, when it became very cold and the snow covered the ground and the great lake was frozen solid, the critters would sit warm and cozy inside the commodious box elder, and pull out the pages written about the boys and read them again and again to each other. Each critter had his favorite among the boys, and he would read particularly from the pages of that boy, and all the room would laugh and hoot and holler and sound amazingly like the boys themselves.

HEN THEY READ and reread the stories, others would say things like, "Read the part again where the six boys tipped the canoe over trying to race the Labrador!"

Or they might implore, "No, no—tell the one about the time they put Miss Hazel (the chocolate Lab) behind the steering wheel and tried to teach her to drive the car by putting a steak bone on a fishing pole and hanging it over the hood!!"

MORE PEELS OF laughter and thigh-slapping as the critters tumbled off their logs and rolled on the floor with their paws kicking spasmodically in the air. Or, "Remember the time they put so and so on the raft with a fishnet and told him to catch the golf balls that seven of them fired at him as fast as they could swat the balls!" Of course, none of the boys on the raft would chicken out and jump in the lake because this was a test of bravery, and chickenry was certain to be followed by the aforementioned merciless derision.

AFTER THE STORY about the raft, the critters would get up and imitate the hapless boy with the fishnet, which produced even more hysterical convulsions from the furry assembly.

One critter laughed so hard when he tried to get through the stories he couldn't breathe and this turned out to be an infectious condition which spread unchecked until the entire room full of critters was completely undone and wholly incapacitated by the intoxication of it all—and the rest of the evening was hopelessly lost to this addictive behavior. In fact, the critters had as much fun telling and retelling these stories as the boys had performing them, and the critters began to think this new site for the box elder was just about right. It was so right, in fact, that the elders had no intention of ever moving to a new site anywhere.

$\mathcal{A}$ND SOMETIMES, IF you look closely through the mist, you can even see the critters and their friends who have become so at ease with their surroundings as to gather around the box elder and its nearby wooded cousins to discuss the latest human observations, or the tiny fox reports, or other peninsula news without any concern that they may be spotted by their own subjects.

It now seems almost certain that they will never leave again, subject to just one small but important caveat, and that caveat is that the boys must come back, and back, and back. Because if they should not come back, the critters would be so saddened that it would break their hearts, and one by one, they would wander off in the dead of the winter's gloomiest nights never to be seen again in the saintly box elder.

And that would break, as well, the hearts of the grownups who live in the nearby red house and love both the boys and the critters and are wholly convinced that when the sun peaks through the clouds momentarily, as it does on even the peninsula's most overcast days, that it is winking at the boys and the critters. This, they say, is how it chooses to indulge itself in its happiest moments as it wends its way through eternity.

$\mathfrak{S}$O IT IS NOW up to the boys and later will be up to the boys' boys and still later their children's children to see that these important bonds endure forever in the rhythms and legends of the mystical peninsula. And this they must do by returning every summer to the little red house that sits in front of the hill that the box elder stands on so elegantly and proudly, and next to the shrine that the critters sit under on quiet nights and watch the stars with their cast of millions and the aurora borealis with its changing colors in equal number—and sometimes, even the sunrise with its cast of one.

To be continued . . .

Postscript

A Near Virtual Perception of Actual Events

The Little Red House

Sunset on the Great Inland Lake

The Critters' Own Subjects Whom They Spied on Summer by Summer

Epilogue

SOME PEOPLE SAY that every story creates itself and then finds a medium to write it. If that is not always true, it is certainly true here. Some thirty years ago, I spent my summers visiting a small cottage on the peninsula next to an open field that had a tree that seemed almost certainly to be magic. Just how many centuries it had survived I never knew, but it was spreading and grand and gnarled from all its experiences.

And it appeared to me that the tree spoke to the critters and the people who happened by it as it swayed in the wind. So in the evenings as the sun was sitting, I would sit in a peeling, red Adirondack chair and listen to it speak to me.

Many years later, I moved away (but not too far) and I would return religiously to visit with the tree that I knew would always be there. Then one day when I went to visit, it was lying on the ground from a roaring storm of the night before. And at that precise moment, the government man came along with this chain saw to cut it up and dispose of it. It seemed unthinkable to see this wonderful, generous tree ending its existence by being carted off to a dump. I thought then and think still today that the tree was speaking to me and making as good sense as I had ever heard.

So I asked the government man if he wouldn't leave it and I would find some way to make other arrangements, which he readily agreed to do. For eight weeks the tree lay there with its sign attached with red tape explaining its circumstances until the arrangements were in place and the tree could be moved—all 8,000 pounds of it.

The boys in the story too thought the tree was spirited and made over it enormously. So I wrote a story about the tree thinking it would be a good thing to read at the dinner table every summer when the boys returned—a sort of annual welcoming ceremony! And as I was doing this, it turned out to be a story about the peninsula and the critters and the boys, as well as the tree—and I was certain that the tree was behind all of this.

When I read it the first time to the boys that still remained that summer, they agreed it needed illustrations and one of their number seemed just right for this. He had decided as a junior in college, with one semester of art training, that that was for him. So when this project was suggested, he jumped at it. An artist without portfolio is a very lonely soul—and this then became his very first project. Having grown up with the peninsula, the man, the boys and the tree, everything seemed to fall in place. And he composed the pictures which matched the words which matched the ancient, wizened tree—and these are the images which now fill the story.

I am almost certain the tree is still speaking as I write this and it gladdens my heart every time I look at it—which I hope will be for a long time.

❧ *Tom Shoaff*

Illustrator, Matthew-John Shoaff

Prints of art work available at *www.foxtalepublishing.com*